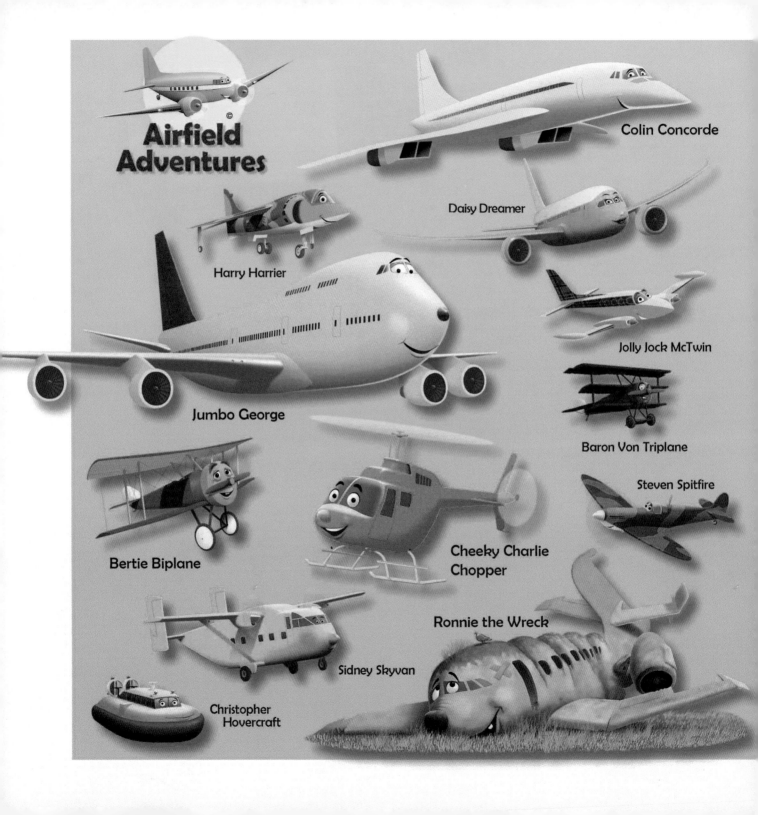

Airfield Adventures

Colin Concorde

Daisy Dreamer

Harry Harrier

Jolly Jock McTwin

Jumbo George

Baron Von Triplane

Steven Spitfire

Bertie Biplane

Cheeky Charlie Chopper

Ronnie the Wreck

Sidney Skyvan

Christopher Hovercraft

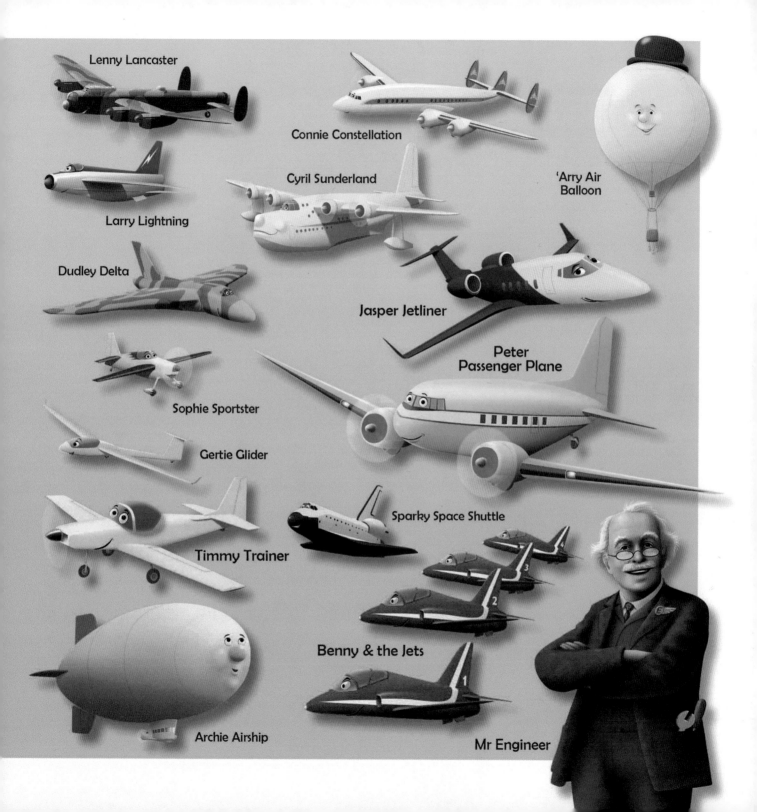

Lenny Lancaster

Connie Constellation

'Arry Air Balloon

Larry Lightning

Cyril Sunderland

Dudley Delta

Jasper Jetliner

Peter Passenger Plane

Sophie Sportster

Gertie Glider

Timmy Trainer

Sparky Space Shuttle

Benny & the Jets

Archie Airship

Mr Engineer

Published by Airfield Adventures Ltd.

www.airfieldadventures.com

Copyright © 2014 Philip Martin-Dye

Airfield Adventures series © 1998

ISBN 978 0 9926526 2 3

Airfield Adventures

Ronnie the Wreck Saves The Day

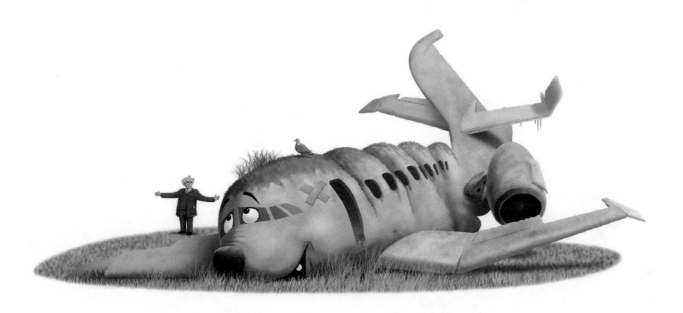

By Captain Philip Martin-Dye

Illustrated by Robin Davies

Many years ago, Ronnie crashed at the Airfield. The damage was so bad that it would have cost too much to repair him. Instead, he was left where he was, just to one side of the runway. He's been there ever since. To most people, the only useful purpose Ronnie serves is to give the airfield firemen a chance to practise their fire drills.... but the other aeroplanes know better! Ronnie the Wreck is their friend, and even though the fire engines spray him with foam every day, he is always happy and smiling, and never complains.

One day, Ronnie was watching the other aeroplanes taking off and landing, as he always did. Suddenly, he noticed that something was wrong with Jasper Jetliner, who was coming in to land. Ronnie had watched all the aeroplanes take off and land so many times that he knew each one's technique by heart, and something was definitely wrong with Jasper's approach to land.

"Oh dear," thought Ronnie, "Jasper should have lowered his undercarriage by now. He must have forgotten. If he lands with his wheels up, he'll crash, and he could finish up a wreck like me."

Jasper was getting nearer and nearer to the runway and still his wheels were not down, but Ronnie didn't know how to warn Jasper. "Even if I shout, he'll never hear me above the noise of his jet engines," thought Ronnie.

Just then, Ronnie noticed Cheeky Charlie Chopper, the helicopter. Charlie was practising his hovering nearby.

"Charlie, we have to stop Jasper landing," shouted Ronnie. "He's forgotten to put his wheels down. We have no time to lose!"

Jasper was getting nearer and nearer to the runway. He would surely crash-land at any moment. Charlie had to think quickly!

"Leave it to me!" shouted Charlie, who instantly whizzed over to where Jasper was going to land, and hovered just above the runway.

Jasper was just about to land when he saw that Charlie was blocking the runway. Immediately, Jasper applied full power to his jet engines and started climbing back into the sky. He was really quite annoyed.

"What on earth is Charlie Chopper thinking about?" thought Jasper to himself. "Fancy blocking the runway when he could see I was about to land!"

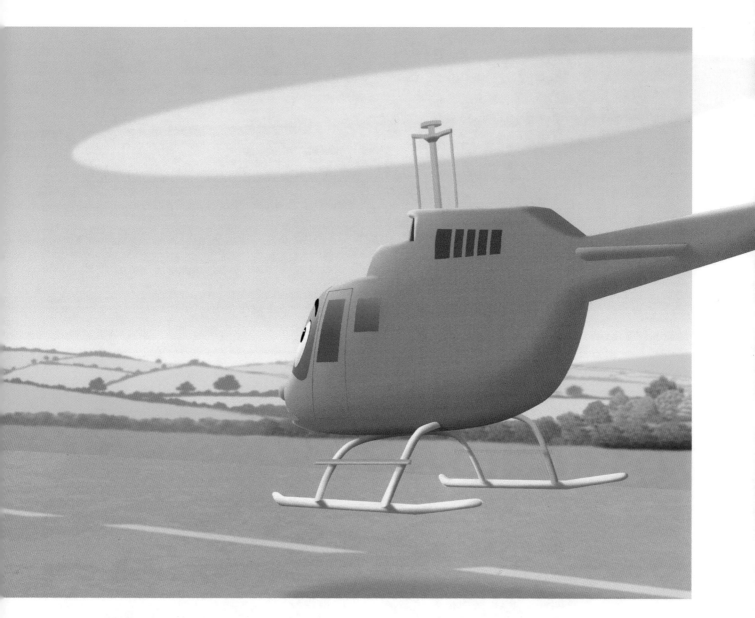

Jasper Jetliner went through his 'Go-around' checks. "Full power applied - checked. Flaps retracting - checked. Undercarriage up..." Jasper went numb with shock.

"Undercarriage up..." he repeated to himself. "But it was never down! That's what Charlie was trying to do! He was trying to stop me landing with my wheels up!"

Jasper circled round for another approach to land. This time he put his wheels down early, and made a safe landing. Jasper was quite shaken. He taxied over to Charlie.

"Thank you Charlie," he stammered. "Your quick thinking saved me from a crash-landing."

"It's not me you need to thank," replied Charlie. "Thank Ronnie the Wreck! He was the one who was keeping an eye on you."

Jasper immediately went over to see Ronnie.

"Thank you Ronnie," he said. "You saved my life."

"That's OK Jasper," replied Ronnie, "I may not be able to fly anymore, but if I can help my friends, then that makes me very happy."

By now, Mr Engineer and all the other aeroplanes had heard what had happened. They came over to thank Ronnie, and to congratulate him. Mr Engineer spoke.

"Ahem!... Ronnie, on behalf of all the aeroplanes, we would like to thank you for saving Jasper Jetliner today. If it wasn't for your endless patience and dedication, Jasper might have become another wreck like you. Sometimes you may think that we don't notice you are there, but we all appreciate you very much. You are indeed a wonderful friend to us all."

Everyone cheered.

Ronnie felt very proud. He was choked with emotion.

"I just love being here with all my friends," he said, "I'm a very lucky aeroplane."

"And we're very lucky too," said Peter Passenger Plane. And everyone cheered again.

That night, all the aeroplanes slept soundly. They were all very happy.

Especially Ronnie the Wreck, who was a very proud aeroplane.

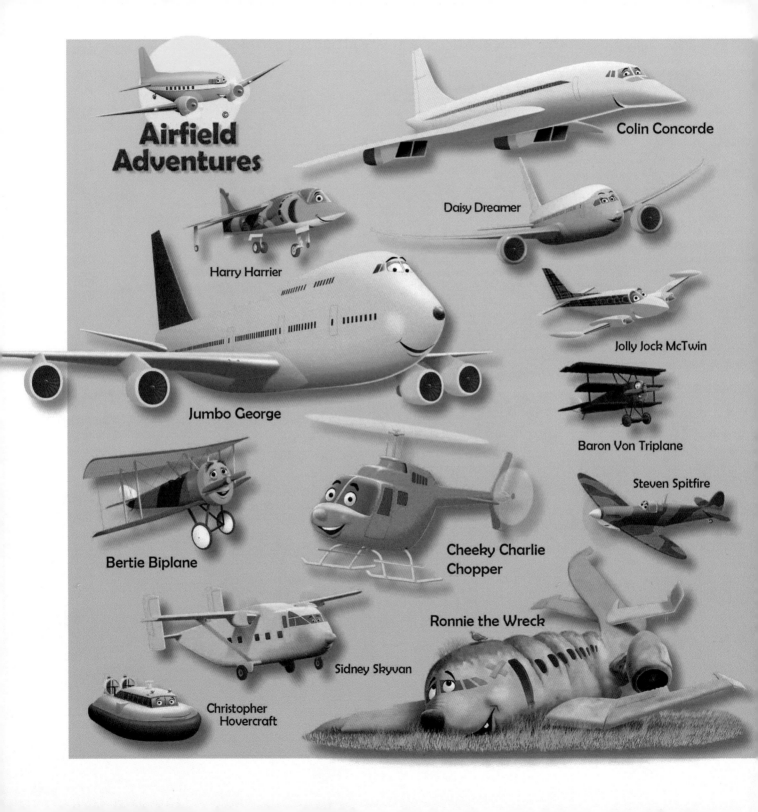

Airfield Adventures

Colin Concorde

Daisy Dreamer

Harry Harrier

Jolly Jock McTwin

Jumbo George

Baron Von Triplane

Bertie Biplane

Cheeky Charlie Chopper

Steven Spitfire

Ronnie the Wreck

Sidney Skyvan

Christopher Hovercraft

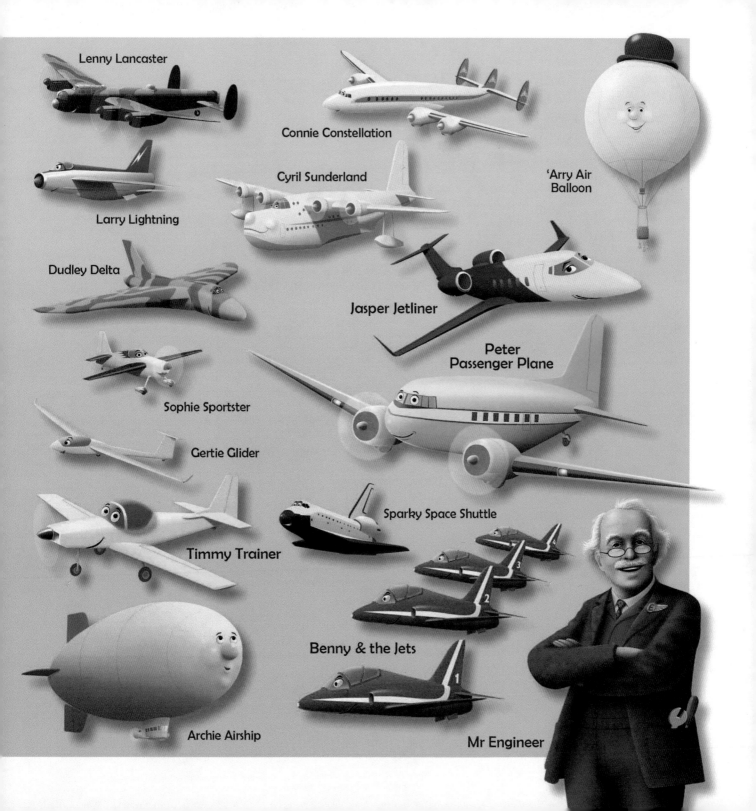

Lenny Lancaster

Connie Constellation

'Arry Air Balloon

Larry Lightning

Cyril Sunderland

Dudley Delta

Jasper Jetliner

Peter Passenger Plane

Sophie Sportster

Gertie Glider

Timmy Trainer

Sparky Space Shuttle

Benny & the Jets

Archie Airship

Mr Engineer

9514437R00016

Printed in Great Britain
by Amazon.co.uk, Ltd.,
Marston Gate.